"Let them give thanks to the LORD for his unfailing love and his wonderful deeds for mankind,
for he satisfies the thirsty and fills the hungry with good things."—Psalm 107:8–9

W9-AVH-464

ZONDERKIDZ

The Berenstain Bears® Give Thanks
Copyright © 2009 by Berenstain Publishing, Inc.
Illustrations © 2009 by Berenstain Publishing, Inc.

The Berenstain Bears® Thanksgiving Blessings
Copyright © 2013 by Berenstain Publishing, Inc.
Illustrations © 2013 by Berenstain Publishing, Inc.

Requests for information should be addressed to:

Zonderkidz, 3900 Sparks Drive SE, Grand Rapids, Michigan 49546

ISBN: 978-0-310-72955-6

Editor: Mary Hassinger
Art direction: Cindy Davis

Printed in China

18 19 20 21 22 23 24 • 7 6 5 4 3 2 1

The Berenstain Bears®
Give Thanks

written by Jan and Mike Berenstain

ZONDERkidz

Living Lights™
A Faith Story

It was autumn in Bear Country, and the sights and the sounds of the season were all around. The leaves on the trees were turning orange, red, and gold. There was a nip in the air, and the sky was a brilliant blue. Flocks of geese flew overhead honking their way south for the winter. Out in his cornfield, Farmer Ben was up on his big red tractor harvesting his crop.

Papa, Brother, and Sister Bear waved to him as they drove up the long drive to the farm. Papa was delivering some new furniture for Mrs. Ben. It was a fine new kitchen table and chairs.

Ben climbed down from his tractor and went to meet them at the farmhouse. Papa and the cubs unloaded the table and chairs and carried them inside. Mrs. Ben was pleased.

"My, don't they look nice!" she said. "It brightens the place up a bit. They do make my curtains look a mite shabby, though. I guess it's time I made some new ones."

"Thank you, Papa Bear," said Ben, shaking hands. "A job well done! Now, about our little deal ..."

The cubs wondered what "deal" Ben was talking about.

"I told you that you could have the pick of my produce in payment for the furniture," said Ben.

"That's right, Ben," said Papa as he nodded. "I was thinking of a few cases of your extra-special, grade-A, apple-blossom honey." Papa licked his lips just thinking about all that delicious honey.

"That's fine," agreed Ben. "You're welcome to it. And I have something else behind the barn that I think might interest you."

"Meet Squanto," said Ben, "my tom turkey. Isn't he a beaut?" Squanto was, indeed, a magnificent bird. He was enormous with a huge fanned tail and glowing colors of black, red, and gold.

"Wow!" said Papa, impressed. "That's some turkey!"

"He's beautiful!" said Sister. "But why is he called 'Squanto'?"

"That was the name of the Native Bear who helped the Pilgrims plant their corn when they settled in their new home," explained Ben. "Squanto celebrated the first Thanksgiving with them after their harvest. I couldn't think of a better name for a turkey."

"He sure is a fine bird," said Papa. "But what's he got to do with my furniture?"

"He's yours if you want him," said Ben. "He'll make you the best Thanksgiving dinner in all Bear Country."

Papa's eyes brightened. "Roast turkey—mmm-*mmm*!"

"Thanksgiving dinner?" said Sister, getting upset. "But that means ..."

"Now don't you fret, Sister Bear," soothed Ben. "Squanto can stay here till Thanksgiving. I'll fatten him up and deliver him all ready for your mama to cook on Thanksgiving morning.

"What do you say, Papa? Is it a deal?"

"It's a deal, Ben!" said Papa, and they shook hands on it. Papa was already imagining that mouth-watering Thanksgiving dinner—roast turkey with stuffing, two kinds of potatoes, gravy, green beans, and squash. Then dessert—pumpkin pie with whipped cream, and maybe some ice cream on top. Yum!

But Sister Bear wasn't so sure she liked the sound of all this. She had never met her Thanksgiving dinner before. It made things more personal. And Squanto was such a beautiful bird. She liked him a lot.

"You know, Papa," she said as they drove home, "I don't think having Squanto for Thanksgiving dinner is such a good idea. I think he would make a nice pet."

"A pet?" said Papa in surprise. "Who ever heard of a turkey for a pet?"

"Why not?" asked Sister. "Lots of cubs have unusual pets. Barry Bruin has a raccoon. Lizzie Bruin has a goat. And Too-Tall Grizzly has a snake. Why couldn't I have a turkey?"

Papa thought of that roast turkey Thanksgiving dinner with all the trimmings.

"Turkeys just don't make good pets," he said. "And that's all there is to it!"

But Sister still didn't like the idea of Squanto being a Thanksgiving dinner.

The weeks went past, and the leaves fell from the trees. The wind grew positively chilly, and one day, a few flakes of snow fell. Thanksgiving was drawing near.

Every day, Sister visited Squanto at the farm. He was growing fatter and finer. His feathers were bright and glossy. When he spread his tail, he looked like a big black, red, and gold peacock. But the closer it got to Thanksgiving, the sadder Sister got. She liked Squanto more and more each day.

Mama noticed that Sister was down in the dumps.

"You know, Sister," said Mama, putting her arm around her shoulder, "Papa's right—turkeys don't make very good pets. They aren't like dogs or cats. You can't play with them or run and jump with them. They're really just farm animals."

"I know," Sister sighed. "But I still like Squanto. He's so pretty."

Mama grew thoughtful. She saw that Sister was really serious about this.

"Now, dear, don't worry about it," she said. "Papa and I will talk it over and I'm sure we can work out something."

Sister brightened up. "Really?" she said. "You mean we won't have Squanto for Thanksgiving dinner?"

"We shall see what we shall see," Mama said, smiling. "And, in the meantime, I have a surprise for you. I've been thinking we should make this Thanksgiving into something extra special. Grizzly Gramps and Gran, Uncle Wilbur, Aunt Min, and Cousin Fred will be coming over for dinner. I thought we could put on a show for them."

"A show?" said Sister, looking excited. She loved putting on a show. "What kind of show?"

"I thought the story of the first Thanksgiving would be appropriate," said Mama. "It could tell all about how the Pilgrims and the Native Bears celebrated the first Thanksgiving together hundreds of years ago."

"Neat!" said Sister. "Will we have costumes?"

"Of course," said Mama. "We can make them ourselves. I have lots of old fabric
we can use. But we'll need feathers for the Native Bears' headdresses."

"Squanto dropped lots of tail feathers," said Sister. "They're perfect! I've been
saving them."

She ran upstairs to get her collection of turkey tail feathers. She brought them
down to Mama's sewing room. Mama had the *P* book from the Bear Encyclopedia
open to *Pilgrims* so she could see what their clothes looked like.

"You're right, dear," said Mama, taking the feathers. "These are perfect. But do you know what else we'll need?"

Sister shook her head.

"We'll need a script for the play," said Mama. "Why don't you write one?"

"Me?"

"Certainly," said Mama, getting out her fabric and spreading it out. "You know the story of the first Thanksgiving, don't you?"

"I guess so," said Sister. She had heard about it in school over and over again every November. She should know it pretty well by now.

"Well, there you are," mumbled Mama, her mouth full of pins as she started work.

So, Sister got out a pad of paper and a pencil and set to work. It was hard. She had never written a play before. She asked Brother for help. Sister wrote the script, and Brother copied the parts for each player. Sister was so busy working on the play that she forgot all about Squanto the turkey for a while.

When Thanksgiving Day finally arrived, everything was ready. The script was written and copied, Mama had sewn beautiful Pilgrim and Native Bear costumes, and the tree house was full of the wonderful smells of Thanksgiving dinner.

Around two o'clock, Grizzly Gramps and Gran, Uncle Wilbur, Aunt Min, and Cousin Fred arrived. Sister and Brother grabbed Fred and took him up to their room to rehearse. Fred had a part in the play too.

An hour later, just before dinnertime, Sister made an appearance on the landing of the stairs. She was dressed as a Pilgrim maiden.

"May I have your attention, please?" she called.

The grown-ups all turned toward her. "Oh, isn't she darling!" said Aunt Min. Sister did look very cute in her Pilgrim maiden hat.

"We will now present *The Story of the First Thanksgiving!*" she announced. The grown-ups all applauded and found their seats to watch the play.

All the grown-ups clapped and stamped and whistled. It was a big hit! Aunt Min wiped her eyes. "They're all so darling!" she sniffed.

Mama rang a bell in the doorway. "Dinnertime!" she called.

"Yea!" cried the cubs as they ran for the dining room. But then, Sister stopped short.

"Oh, no!" she said. "What about my turkey, Squanto? I forgot all about him! What happened to Squanto?"

"Don't worry, Sister," said Papa, leading her to the window. "Squanto is safe and sound. I decided that turkeys do make good pets after all!"

And there, in his own brand-new pen in the Bears' own backyard, was Squanto. His tail was spread proudly, and he looked very pleased with himself.

"Oh, Squanto!" said Sister, very happy. "Welcome to your new home!"

The Bear family all gathered around the dining table. Everything was just as Papa had imagined it—two kinds of potatoes, stuffing and gravy, corn on the cob and corn muffins, green beans, pumpkin pie with whipped cream, and ice cream too. But, in the center of the table, instead of a roast turkey, there was a magnificent honey-baked salmon.

"MMM-*MMM*!" said all the bears.

Then it was time to say grace. The Bear family held hands and bowed their heads. Grizzly Gramps, as the eldest of the clan, said the prayer.

"Dear Lord, we give thanks for all your blessings—for this great feast that you have provided, for the warm homes that give us shelter, for the love of our family that surrounds us today, and for all the beauties of the earth that you in your great love and wisdom have created. Amen!"

"Amen!" everyone said, picking up their knives and forks.

But Sister had something to add.
"And I am especially thankful for my wonderful new pet, Squanto the turkey!"

"AMEN!" everyone said again. And they all laughed.

"Men!" echoed Honey as they dug into that delicious food like a family of hungry bears.

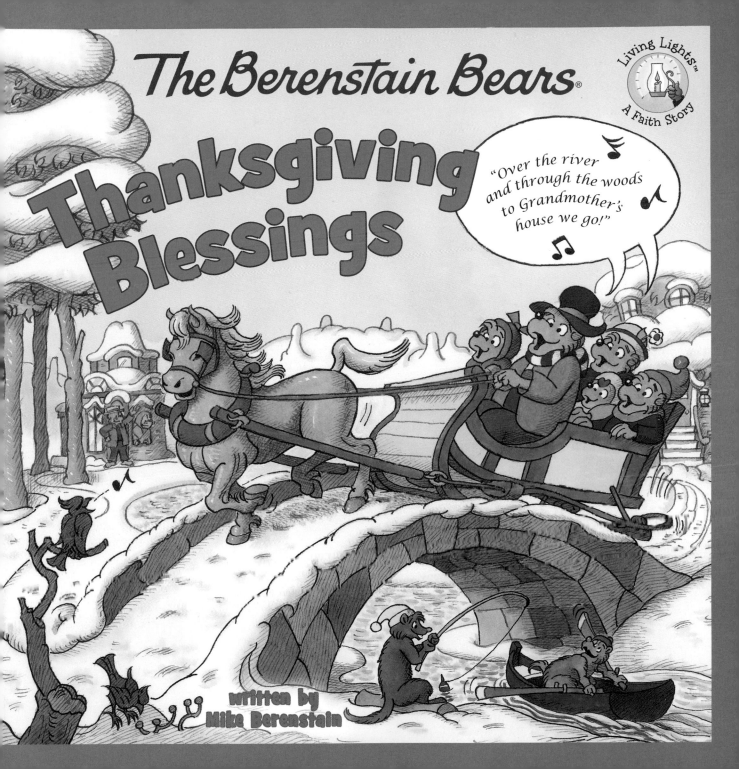

It was autumn in Bear country, and Thanksgiving Day was here. But an early snowstorm was making things look more like Christmas. Instead of bright fall colors, the leaves of the Bear family's tree house were covered with new-fallen snow.

The Bears were going to Grizzly Gramps' and Gran's for Thanksgiving dinner. It would take more than a snowstorm, early or otherwise, to keep them away from Gran's wonderful cooking. Papa decided to borrow Farmer Ben's horse and sleigh to make the trip. They would travel in style through the snowy countryside.

As they set off, the bears crossed a little bridge over a stream. "It's just like the old song," said Sister.

Over the river and through the woods
to Grandmother's house we go.
The horse knows the way
to carry the sleigh
through the white and drifted ...

"Snow!"

"I can't wait for Thanksgiving dinner!" said Brother.

"Me, neither," said Sister.

"Neither!" yelled Honey.

"I have to agree with you," said Papa, smacking his lips. "Think of all Gran's delicious Thanksgiving dishes—roast turkey with chestnut stuffing …"

"Gravy and cranberry sauce …" added Brother.

"Sweet potatoes and mashed potatoes …" sighed Sister.

"Apple pie and pumpkin pie …" went on Mama.

"Pie!" yelled Honey.

"Of course," said Mama, "there's more to Thanksgiving Day than just eating lots of yummy food."

"Yes, indeed," said Papa. "It's a time for giving thanks and thinking of all our blessings."

"Like the blessing of food?" asked Sister.

"Well …" said Papa, "there are many other Thanksgiving blessings to remember. For instance, the blessings of faith and freedom."

"What do you mean?" asked Brother.

"We should remember those first Pilgrim Bears who came to Bear Country long ago," explained Papa. "They were seeking a land where they could worship God in freedom. At first, life was hard in the new land. But the Native Bears, who already lived here, gave them food and shared in a great feast. That was the first Thanksgiving. Those Pilgrims gave us the freedom to have faith and worship God in whatever way we think is right."

"After the time of the Pilgrims, many others traveled here to find freedom. They farmed the land and made it bloom. It was a rich and fruitful place. Then enemies came from across the sea and tried to take it all away. There was war and suffering. But peace came, at last, and the land was safe. We should all be thankful for the blessings of peace and plenty too."

Peace and Plenty

"With peace and plenty, the country grew. Roads, cities, bridges, and workshops were built. Boats sailed the rivers as wagons and trains crossed the land. There was work to be done. And when that work was finished, there was time for play. There were fairs and shows, dances and games, singing and music. These are the blessings of work and play."

Work and Play

"Now our whole Bear family lives here in this blessed land. We are safe in our snug tree house home. We can celebrate Thanksgiving with Gramps and Gran. We have good neighbors to depend on like Farmer and Mrs. Ben. And those are the most wonderful blessings of all—the blessings of family and friends."

Family and Friends

"Wow!" said Brother, as the sleigh came out of the woods. "I never realized we had so much to be thankful for."

"Yes," said Sister, "and we can also be thankful that we're finally getting close to Grizzly Gramps' and Gran's house."

The whole family sang:

"Over the river and through the woods, now grandmother's cap I spy! Hurrah for the fun! Is the pudding done? Hurrah for the pumpkin pie!"

"Pie!" yelled Honey.

"Pie!"

"But Gran doesn't have a cap," said Sister. "She has a scarf."

"Well, I spy it anyway—through the kitchen window," said Brother.

As the sleigh pulled up, Gramps came out to greet them.

"Hello, there, young'uns!" he said, squeezing the cubs in a big bear hug. "Are you ready for our great Thanksgiving feast?"

"Yes, Gramps," said Sister. "But, you know, we should also think about all our Thanksgiving blessings."

"I always do!" said Gramps, leading them inside and into the kitchen. "And the Thanksgiving blessing I think about most is Grizzly Gran, herself—the best cook in Bear Country!"

"Now, Gramps," scolded Gran. "Stop your nonsense and help get the food on."

The whole family helped set the table. It was, indeed, a magnificent Thanksgiving feast.

"It's a shame there aren't any Native Bears here to share it with us," said Brother.

"Never fear," said Gramps, seating himself at the head of the table. "My great, great grandmother was one-quarter Native Bear and I am ready to share. Let's eat!"

"Aren't you forgetting something, Gramps?" reminded Gran.
"Yes, of course," said Gramps.
They all joined hands and bowed their heads.

"Thank you, Lord, for all your Thanksgiving blessings," prayed
Gramps. "Thank you for the blessings of faith and freedom, of peace
and plenty, of work and play, and of family and friends. And …" he
added, "thank you for our wonderful Thanksgiving feast! Amen."

"Amen!" said all the bears.

"And now," said Gramps, picking up his knife and fork, "let's eat!"